The Berenstain Bears
and the
IN-CROWD

One's sense of self-worth
is often undone
the first time one feels
left out of the fun.

A First Time Book®

The Berenstain Bears
and the

Stan & Jan Berenstain

IN-CROWD

Random House New York

Library of Congress Cataloging-in-Publication Data: Berenstain, Stan. The Berenstain bears and the in-crowd. (A First time book) SUMMARY: A rich new cub named Queenie McBear teases Sister Bear and steals her Double-Dutch partners away before the big tournament. [1. Conduct of life—Fiction. 2. Rope skipping—Fiction. 3. Bears—Fiction] I. Jan, Berenstain. II. Title. III. Series: Berenstain, Stan. First time books. PZ7.B4483Bejl 1989 [E] 88-32095 ISBN: 0-394-83013-X (pbk.); 0-394-93013-4 (lib. bdg.)

Manufactured in the United States of America 1 2 3 4 5 6 7 8 9 0

It was early summer in Bear Country. School had been out for a few weeks, and Brother and Sister Bear had settled into a comfortable routine of bike riding, playing ball, exploring, and just generally having fun.

They had chores, of course—keeping their room neat, helping with yard cleanup, and, when he got very busy, helping Papa Bear in his shop. Mostly, though, they were looking forward to a carefree summer of fun and relaxation.

But sometimes the road ahead is not as smooth as we would like. Sometimes there are unexpected potholes in the road of life, and Sister Bear, as it turned out, was headed for a real wheel-buster.

With school closed, the playground was the gathering place for Brother, Sister, and the neighborhood cubs. It had swings and slides, a jungle gym, a track, and a sandbox for little cubs. There were also jump ropes, Frisbees, and soccer balls you could get from Miss Mack, who was in charge.

On most days Sister would stop off
for her best friend, Lizzy Bruin, and
they would go to the playground together.
After a swing and a slide or two they
would get a jump rope from Miss Mack.
Lately, they had been getting two ropes
for Double Dutch.

In Double Dutch, the jumper jumps over two ropes that are being turned in opposite directions. It isn't easy, but Sister and Lizzy and some of their friends had been practicing and were getting pretty good at it.

That's what was happening the day
the trouble started. Sister and Lizzy had
two ropes and were looking for other cubs to
join them. But where *was* everybody? Where
were Anna, Millie, and Linda, their usual
jumpmates? As they looked around they spied
a small crowd at the far corner of the playground
near the bike rack. That's when Anna ran by.

"How about a little Double Dutch?" called Sister.

"Can't now!" shouted Anna. "There's a new cub with
a terrific ten-speed bike
and she's letting us take
turns riding it!"

It sounded interesting, and even though
Sister and Lizzy were still a bit small for
two-wheelers, they decided to investigate.
The new cub not only had a pretty sharp bike—
it was purple and had ten speeds and hand
brakes—she was pretty sharp herself. She
wore purple stretch pants, a designer top, a
yellow headband, and hoop earrings.

"Her name's Queenie McBear," whispered Anna,
"and she just moved into the neighborhood. She
has *pierced ears*!"

Sister pushed through the crowd, gave the newcomer, who was taller than she was and a little older, a big smile, and said, "Hi! I'm Sister Bear!" Queenie smiled too, but it wasn't exactly friendly.

"Sister Bear?" she said. "Now what kind of a name is that? And you've got to be kidding with those clothes—a pink ruffled jumper and a *hair bow*?"

"Well..." said Sister, a little confused. "It's *my* kind of name. And as for my clothes..."

"Why don't you and your little friend go play in the sandbox?" interrupted Queenie, not giving Sister a chance to finish. Then she got on her bike and shouted, "Come on, gang! Let's go to the Dairy Bear for some soft ice cream! My treat!" And off she zoomed down the road.

Jumpmates Anna, Millie, and Linda looked a little embarrassed, but soft ice cream was soft ice cream, so they got on their bikes with the rest and followed Queenie down the road.

Now Sister was very confused—
and upset, too.

"I don't get it," said Lizzy.
"All you did was say hi...Say, I know
what," she added, trying to cheer
her up, "I heard that Miss Mack is
organizing a Double-Dutch tournament
with prizes and everything! Come on!
Let's go sign up!"

Sister Bear didn't even answer.
She was so upset that she just turned
and went home.

She was usually so cheerful after a session at the playground that it didn't take long for Mama Bear to figure out that something must have gone wrong. Papa and Brother Bear noticed too.

After supper, the whole story of Queenie came out—
her bike, her sharp clothes, and how she'd made fun of
Sister and then treated everybody to soft ice cream.

"Everybody except me and Lizzy," she said glumly.

"What did she make fun of?" asked Mama.

"My name, my clothes, my hair bow...*me!*" said Sister.

"Oh dear," said Mama. "That wasn't very nice, not very nice at all— maybe she was just trying to make an impression."

"Well, she certainly made an impression on me," said Sister. "A *bad* impression."

Of course, Mama had been a cub once and she knew about in-crowds and cubs like Queenie who tried to build themselves up by putting other cubs down. But she also knew that it didn't do much good to stew about it. So she gave Sister a hug and said, "Don't fret, sweetie. I'm sure things will look a lot brighter in the morning."

Things did look a lot brighter in the morning, and Sister Bear was once again her confident self. She decided that today she would ride her trike to the playground. The playground was just as much hers as Queenie's and besides, she wanted to ask Miss Mack about that Double-Dutch tournament. It sounded interesting. And maybe Queenie wouldn't even be there.

Queenie was not only there; she and the gang were riding around the track on their bikes. When Sister tried to join in, all she got for her trouble was a cloud of dust and more of Queenie's smart talk.

"Well, if it isn't Little Miss Hair Bow on her tricycle! Excuse our dust!" she shouted as she whizzed past.

Excuse her dust indeed, thought Sister, getting an idea—I'll show that Queenie McBear! She pedaled home as fast as she could. She hoped Brother Bear wasn't out riding his big two-wheeler, because that was her idea: to borrow his bike, go back, and ride circles around that Queenie McBear.

She managed to get on
Brother's bike by standing
on a step—and she almost
got it going. But her legs
were a little too short,
and after a few wobbly
circles she crashed—
ker-*whomp!*

"Oh dear!" said Mama, who had just returned from a quick shopping trip to the mall and was watching from one of the tree-house windows. She had a pretty good idea that Sister's attempt to ride the two-wheeler had something to do with Queenie and the in-crowd.

"I guess you had another run-in with that new cub," she said as Sister came into the house. "Well, here's a little something to cheer you up." She reached into her shopping bag and took out some new clothes—some new and different clothes for Sister Bear.

There were some very sharp jeans, a green-and-white striped designer top, and a bright green headband.

"For me?" said Sister.

"Of course," said Mama. "Come on, now. Let's try them on. You know," she continued as she helped Sister out of her pink ruffled jumper and polka dot blouse and into her new outfit, "maybe these new things will change your luck."

"Maybe," agreed Sister. But then she asked, "Mama, why did Queenie pick on me like that?"

"Well," said Mama thoughtfully, "sometimes there are cubs, even grownups, who behave that way. They show off for the crowd by picking on someone who has a certain kind of name or wears a certain kind of clothes. They try to build themselves up by putting others down. That's how in-crowds get started."

"But how about Anna, Millie, and Linda?" asked Sister. "They've always been my friends. Why did they side with Queenie?"

"Maybe because they were glad Queenie wasn't picking on *them*—and soft ice cream *is* soft ice cream—there!" she said, removing Sister's pink hair bow and putting on her new headband. "You're all set! Here, have a look at yourself in the big mirror."

"It's very nice," Sister said, "and I really appreciate the new things. But there's one problem: *It's just not me!* I *like* me," she said as she stepped down, "and I wouldn't change me for a whole bunch of Queenie McBears!" Then she took off her new outfit and put her old one back on, hair bow and all. "And she can keep her old in-crowd! Excuse me, Mama. I have to make a phone call." She marched over to the phone and dialed a number.

"Hello, Lizzy," she said. "About that Double-Dutch tournament..."

The Double-Dutch tournament had gotten to be a big thing. A lot of teams signed up. There were even some boy-cub teams. Brother Bear was on one, along with Cousin Fred and the Too-Tall gang. When Sister and Lizzy signed up, Anna, Millie, and Linda quit Queenie's team and joined Sister's. Not only was Sister the best Double Dutcher in the neighborhood, but Anna and the others were getting a little tired of Queenie's snooty ways.

Sister Bear led her team in as fine an exhibition of Double-Dutch jumping as had ever been seen in Bear Country. It was no contest; her team won going away! Queenie's team was a Double-Dutch disaster—especially Queenie, who made the mistake of wearing beads and big hoop earrings that caught in the rope and ended in a terrible tangle.

After the prizes were awarded, the cubs all crowded around and congratulated Sister. They wanted her to teach them some of her Double-Dutch tricks.

As they lined up for lessons, Lizzy called out to Queenie, "How about you?"

"No thanks," said Queenie with a little grin. "I've already learned *my* lesson."